PUT YOUR SHOES ON & GET READY!

By Raphael G. Warnock

Illustrated by TeMika Grooms

PHILOMEL

PHILOMEL BOOKS
An imprint of Penguin Random House LLC, New York

First published in the United States of America by Philomel Books,
an imprint of Penguin Random House LLC, 2023

Visit us online at penguinrandomhouse.com.
Library of Congress Cataloging-in-Publication Data is available.
Manufactured in Italy

ISBN 9780593528877
10 9 8 7 6 5 4 3 2 1

LEG

Edited by Jill Santopolo
Design by Lily K. Qian
Text set in ITC Cheltenham Pro.
Art was done in Photoshop using digital brushes.

The publisher does not have any control over and does not assume any
responsibility for author or third-party websites or their content.

THANK YOU TO MY BOOK AGENT, WILL LIPPINCOTT; TO MY EDITOR,
JILL SANTOPOLO; AND TO VARIAN JOHNSON AND TeMIKA GROOMS
FOR HELPING ME TO MAKE MY STORY COME ALIVE FOR
CHILDREN. —R. G. W.

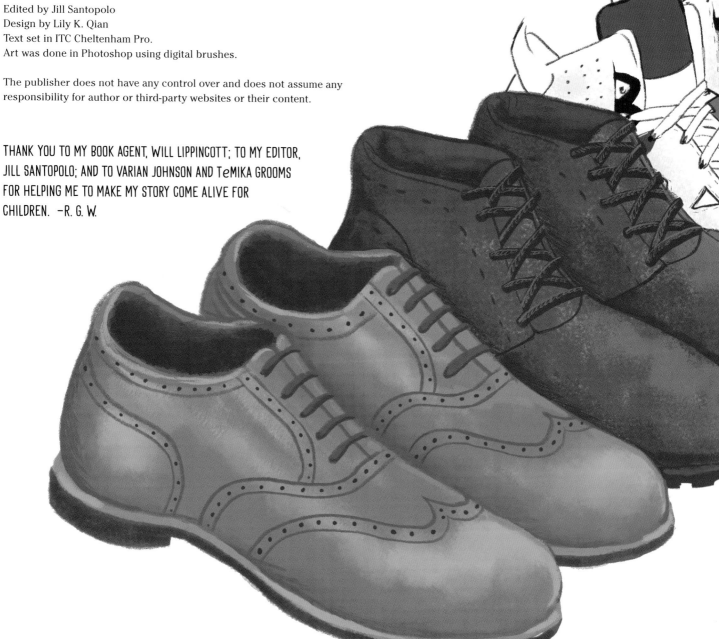

I GOT SHOES, YOU GOT SHOES,

ALL OF GOD'S CHILDREN GOT SHOES!

WHEN I GET TO HEAVEN, GONNA PUT ON MY SHOES;

I'M GONNA WALK ALL OVER GOD'S HEAVEN.

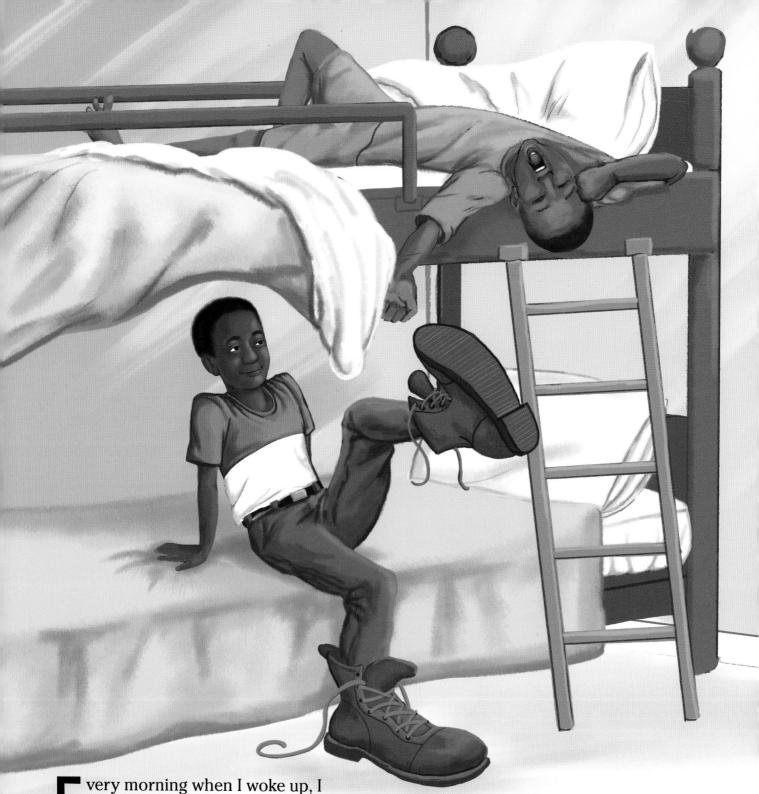

Every morning when I woke up, I
was greeted with very same thing.
It didn't matter if it was a school day
or a Sunday, or whether it was a heat wave
or an ice storm.

"Get up! Get dressed! Get ready!" my dad said.

"For what?" I asked one morning.

"Well, I don't know yet, Raphael," my dad said. "But there's something
for you to do. So put your shoes on and get ready!"

But sometimes I didn't want to put my shoes on. So I put my dad's shoes on instead.

"Nuh-uh, those are for my job," my dad told me. "You've got to put the right shoes on for the work you're meant to do."

During the year, that meant I wore my tennis shoes to school. But in the summer, I wore my boots and worked for my dad's business, hauling rusted cars out of a junkyard to make money for the family.

School year or summer, it didn't matter. My dad always woke
me up the same way: "Get up! Get dressed! Put your shoes on
and get ready!"

During the week, my father lifted broken cars, and on Sundays, he had a different job. As a preacher, he lifted people who felt broken. He saw value in both.

When he put on his stiff shirt, his skinny tie, and his shiny lace-up shoes to give his weekly sermon, I wore my church shoes. I would sit proudly, listening to my father's voice ring out, loud and strong, as he explained how life could be better if everyone loved and helped each other.

I wondered if one day, when I was older, I might wake up on Sundays and put on a stiff shirt, a skinny tie, and shiny lace-up shoes and give weekly sermons just like my dad. But I didn't have the shoes for that job yet. I wasn't ready.

After church came Sunday dinner at the fellowship hall. Everybody had a place at the table, and everybody had their shoes to wear. The chicken and turkey wings, lima beans and collard greens, corn bread and rice filled our stomachs—and being part of a community filled our souls.

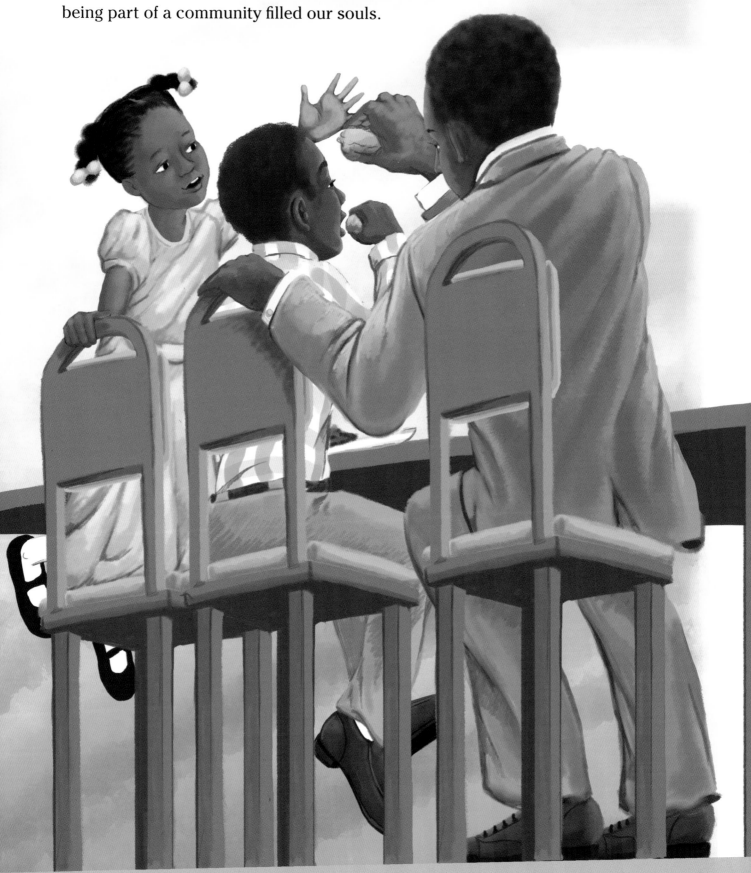

Sometimes the only work I had to do was listen to stories my parents told me. So I wore my slippers.

They told me how when they were children, Black people and white people had to remain separate and couldn't use the same bathrooms or water fountains. They couldn't go to the same schools or play on the same playgrounds. And the ones the white families had were always better. Even though they were just kids, my mom and dad knew this was unfair.

When he was a young man, my dad was drafted into the army. Despite his service to his country, he still wasn't treated fairly. In fact, he was once forced to give up his seat on a bus while he was wearing his soldier's uniform. But he got up every day, got dressed, put his shoes on, and got ready to face what lay head.

When I got older, I watched my brothers play
football. Their cleats were sharp, made for speed.
My sister and the other girls on the flag team wore
their dancing shoes, and my friends cheered them
on from the sidelines, their cheerleading shoes
helping them jump high off the ground.

I wasn't as good of an athlete as my brothers,
but I still played basketball with my friends. I'd
get up, get dressed in my T-shirt and shorts, put
my canvas high-tops on, and get ready. My friends
used to say that I had the ugliest jump shot in
the neighborhood, but thanks to the spring in my
shoes, the basketball still often went in.

When I got even older, I joined the band. I loved game days, when I would get up, put on my uniform and my white marching shoes, and get ready to play my baritone horn.

During halftime, as spectators swayed and sang along to our music, I realized I wasn't scared to be in front of a crowd, and I wasn't shy about being heard.

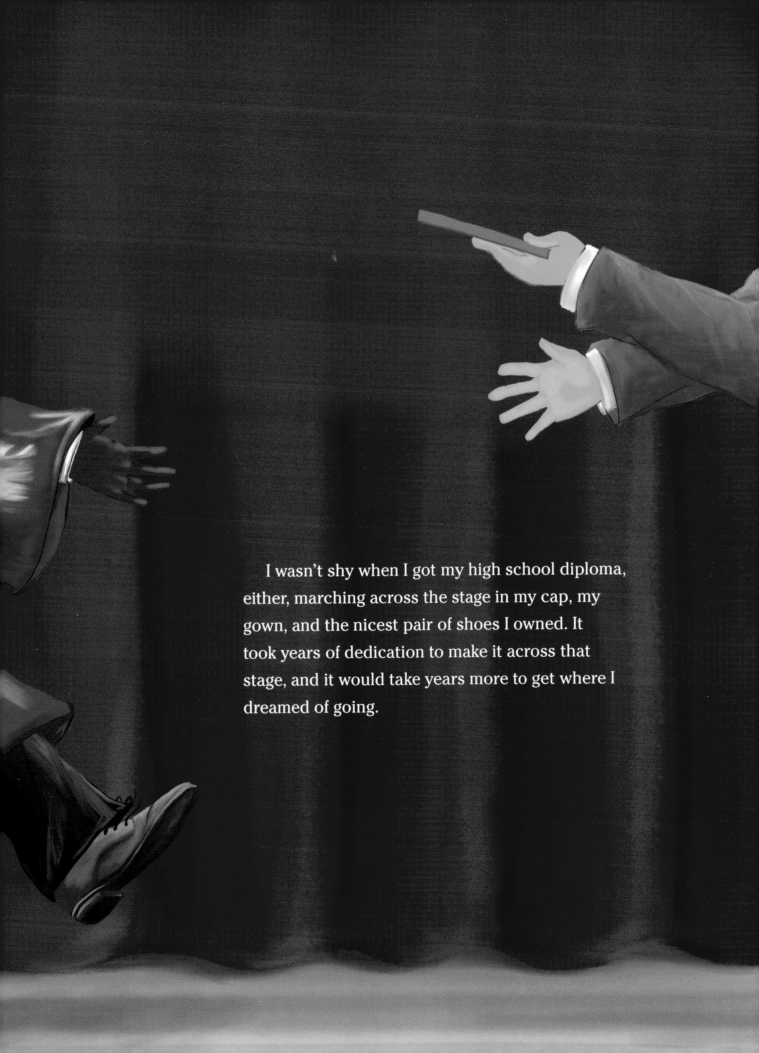

I wasn't shy when I got my high school diploma, either, marching across the stage in my cap, my gown, and the nicest pair of shoes I owned. It took years of dedication to make it across that stage, and it would take years more to get where I dreamed of going.

The first step was attending Morehouse College. I was a little nervous during those first few days on campus, walking around in shoes that pinched my feet, but I knew I wanted to be a preacher—like my father, and like Dr. Martin Luther King Jr., who used his words to inspire people to make the world better . . . for everyone.

So even though my dad was still back home in Savannah, every morning I got up, got dressed, and got myself ready to face the day.

Eventually, I became the senior pastor of Ebenezer Baptist Church—the same church that Dr. King once led. I have been honored to follow in his footsteps. And my father's footsteps, too.

Just like my dad did when I was a little boy, I get up on Sundays, put on my stiff shirt, my tie, and my shiny shoes, and step in front of the congregation to give my weekly sermon.

But while I give sermons like my father and preach from the same pulpit as Dr. King, I never thought it was my job to walk in either of their shoes.

I must wear my own shoes—shoes that fit my feet.

I have to do the job that I was meant to do.

Whether I'm serving breakfast or leading a march, I always wake up, get dressed, put my shoes on, and get ready for the day.

Part of my job is helping others by being an activist. In order to make the world a better place, I have to lead by example.

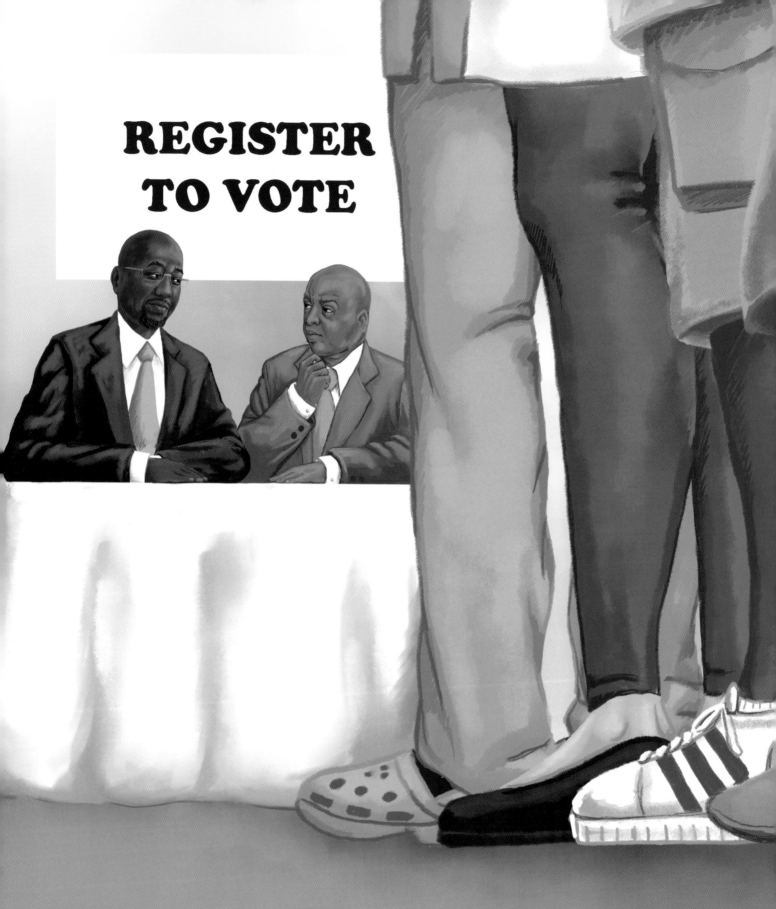

And while I still wear my pastor shoes and my activist shoes, I decided I wanted to try on another pair of shoes, too. I wanted to find another way to help people.

So I decided to run for the United States Senate.

Now, as Georgia's first Black senator, I fight for the people. All the people.

And there are a lot of people counting on me. Depending on me. They need good schools, good jobs, and roads to get to both.

So every morning, I get up, get dressed in my suit and tie with my US Senator pin on my lapel, put my lace-up shoes on, and get ready to fight for people's rights.

Before I leave for work, I try to help my kids put on their shoes. But they prefer to play in mine.

My son stomps around in my boots, while my daughter wears my shoes and ties and proclaims, "I'm Senator Warnock!"

I let them flop around for a while, but they never get very far in my shoes.

Once playtime is over, I help them put on their own shoes—shoes made to fit their feet—and I tell them, just like my dad told me, "You have to put on shoes that fit your feet—shoes for the job you're meant to do."

And that's what I tell all the young people I meet. No matter who you are, where you come from, or what you want to do, there is a job that's right for you. So it's time to get up, get dressed,

PUT YOUR SHOES ON, AND GET READY!